First published in Great Britain in 2013 by Hodder Children's Books

Almost Naked Animals® and associated characters, trademarks
and design elements are owned by 9 Story Entertainment® Inc.
© 2013 9 Story Entertainment® Inc. All Rights Reserved.

Licensed by 9 Story Enterprises Inc.

Written by Claire Sipi, with pages 18-19 and 48-49 by Sarah Courtauld.
Comic strip on pages 32-35 courtesy of Titan Magazines.
Originally published in Totally: Almost Naked Animals Magazine.
Interior layout by ninataradesign.com

I

A Catalogue record for this book is available from the British Library.

ISBN: 978 1 444 91392 7

Printed in China

The paper used in this book is a natural recyclable product made from
wood grown in sustainable forests. The hard coverboard is recycled.

Hodder Children's Books
A division of Hachette Children's Books
338 Euston Road, London NW1 3BH
An Hachette UK company
www.hachette.co.uk

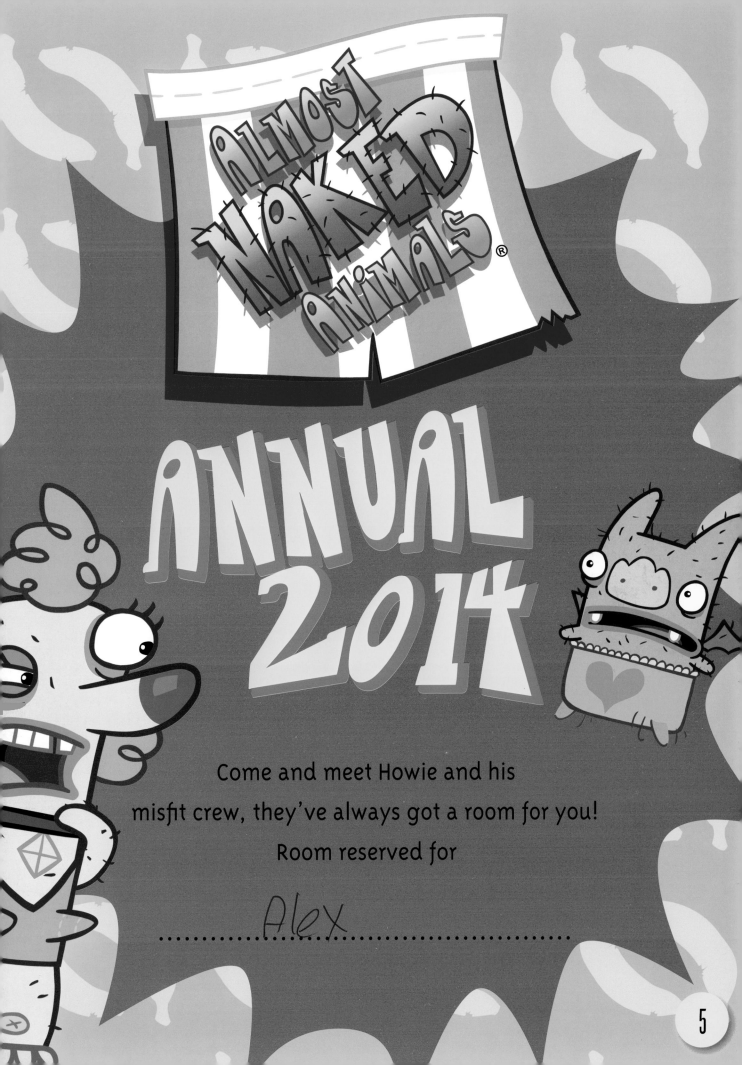

ALMOST NAKED ANIMALS®

ANNUAL 2014

Come and meet Howie and his
misfit crew, they've always got a room for you!
Room reserved for

Alex
....

CONTENTS

HOWIE'S WELCOME

Welcome to the Banana Cabana! Leave your suitcase at the door and get ready for the holiday of a lifetime!

This annual is full of well … Dog Stuff, Octo Stuff, Piggy Stuff, Bunny Stuff, Duck Stuff … and loads of cool activities and side-splitting Cabana adventures with me, Howie, and my awesome friends!

Now, before you join in with our brain-scratching, death-defying (don't worry, Octo has his first aid kit on hand!), super-fun activities in this Cabana-tastic book, here are my super special friends — and me, of course, the world-famous stunt dog …

Turn the page — after all, what could possibly go wrong … ?

Just about everything, if you ask me!

Pssst! For all you Almost Naked Animals Fans out there that like a challenge — like me — keep a look out for: throughout this Annual. Count how many times you see Duck in his Hero Sandwich outfit, and write your answer here:

WARNING! The management regret that they cannot take responsibility for any lost or damaged property!

HOWIE

Manager of the Banana Cabana

Likes: Trampolines, running fast, ear wax

Dislikes: Silence, quitters, bubble baths

Personality: Cheerful, fun-loving, impulsive. I love a challenge, doing stunts, playing games and of course running my hotel. My friends say I'm not that good at planning, but, hey, who needs planning-schmanning when you can have fun instead!

Hero: Dirk Danger

Sister: Poodle

Big Dream: To be a world-famous stunt dog, just like my hero Dirk Danger

Best friend: Octo

and this is my hotel ...

The Banana Cabana

Semi-fine beachfront resort hotel with pool

Star rating: one-star establishment

If you love fun, mayhem and destruction, then this is the hotel for you!

OCTO

Front desk clerk at the Banana Cabana

Likes: Firm mattresses, clean teeth, pop-up books

Dislikes: Slippery floors, most condiments, clowns

Personality: Scaredy-puss, nervous, highly-strung and obsessed with details. Poor Octo is a bit of a panic-boots! He can often be seen jiggling with fear, breathing into a paper bag to try and stop himself from hyperventilating! In spite of all this, Octo is a loyal friend to Howie and joins in with his wacky stunts, even though it goes against his better judgement and he knows it breaks all health and safety rules ... GULP!

Big Dream: To remove all possible causes of danger from any given situation and to make everything safe and sound

Best friend: Howie

BUNNY

Activities Director at the Banana Cabana

Likes: Princesses (proper ones, not ones like Poodle!), stickers, rainbows

Dislikes: Slow days, broken mirrors, armpits

Personality: This bossy bunny has A-T-T-I-T-U-D-E! One minute she's sugary sweet and the next ... well, let's say it's probably a good idea to avoid her and her very short fuse! Bunny has oodles of energy and enthusiasm, but if things don't go her way she gets quite huffy. She wants everything to be perfect, and she certainly makes sure that everyone knows where, when and what she is doing

Big Dream: To live in a perfect world where everything goes her way!

Best friend: Whoever's doing exactly what she says

Ninjitsu Chef at the Banana Cabana

Likes: Ninjitsu, cheese, scooping things

Dislikes: Snow cones, greedy weasels, not scooping things

Personality: No one is quite sure where Piggy comes from, or what he did before he came to work at the Banana Cabana as a master chef, but this serious swine has a secret skill — he is ninjitsu trained! Often heard yelling at his co-workers and the hotel guests, this loud, passionate, pants-wearing pig takes his job very seriously, and often loses his temper. If you don't want a karate chop in the pork chops, best not to get on the wrong side of him, especially in his kitchen where there are plenty of scoopy things …

Big Dream: No one really knows — Ninjitsus are trained not to reveal too much about themselves …

Best friend: No one is brave enough to ask him!

Banana Cabana's handy animal

Likes: Sand castles, lasers, alternate universes

Dislikes: Bread crumbs, cloudy days, itchy feet

Personality: Where do we start? Let's just say that dear Duck lives in his own quackers world, an alternate universe where anything random can happen, and often does! Always willing to try anything, and probably a little over-eager to help, Duck does whatever he is told to do. He may be … unusual, and he may live inside his own shell of oblivion most of the time, but occasionally Duck has a moment of pure genius and exhibits the most unexpected and unusual talents!

Big Dream: Probably beyond anyone but Duck's understanding

Best friend: Everyone and anything!

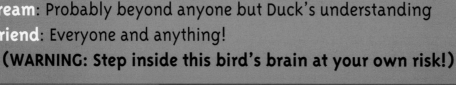

(WARNING: Step inside this bird's brain at your own risk!)

NARWHAL

Resident Performer/Entertainer at the Banana Cabana

Likes: Butter, horn polish, magic and wonder

Dislikes: Green jellybeans, social studies, ring tosses

Personality: Super confident and über-vain, Narwhal is one smooth ol' charmer, who loves the sound of his own voice. When this cheesy crooner isn't wooing the crowds with his buttery voice, then he can usually be found staring at the love of his life (himself!) in the mirror

Big Dream: In his mind he's already achieved it — to be the BEST crooner EVER, with hundreds of adoring fans!

Best friend: Himself, of course!

SLOTH

Bellhop at the Banana Cabana

Likes: Lounging, Howie, Makeovers

Dislikes: Long walks, line dancing, old cheese

Personality: How much time have you got? S-L-O-W and steady, Sloth will get your bags to your room by the time you are leaving the Cabana! But let's be honest, her mind isn't really on her job most of the time, 'cos she's too busy swooning over her crush, Howie (who is oblivious to her adoring looks and sighs!). However insane Howie's plans might be, Sloth oozes with smitten support. Sigh!

Big Dream: To be Howie's GIRLFRIEND — swooooon!

SLOTH 💜 HOWIE

Best friend: Wishes it was Howie, but loves all her bezzies at the Banana Cabana

Manager of the Chateau Chattoo

POODLE

Likes: Fountains, golden bricks, custard

Dislikes: Howie, Howie's friends, uncomfortable chairs

Personality: A prissy 'princess' who cares only (and we mean ONLY) about herself, ALL day EVERY day. This control freak rules her hotel with an iron-manicured paw! In fact, you'll never find Poodle getting her pretty paws dirty, oh no! She gets Batty, her hench-animal, to do all her dirty work for her. Well, it's much more fun that way … mwah ha ha!

Hero: Herself!

Brother: Nobody … OK fine, it's Howie

Big Dream: To take over the Banana Cabana and shut it down

Side-kick: Batty, Poodle's numero uno hench-animal

and this is her hotel …

Chateau Chattoo

Fancy, elite, extra-deluxe, ultra-ritzy resort hotel. Situated across the bay from the Cabana on its own island

Star rating: Currently unknown as stars have escaped! Potentially 6-star establishment, something the manager is very smug about (take note, Howie!)

If you're snooty, love fountains and don't mind being referred to as a pain-in-the-neck by the hotel's snooty owner, then this is the place for you!

Short, jumpy and not very clever, poor ol' Batty will basically do anything his boss asks him to do. He's always going out of his way to serve Poodle's every need and to win her approval (which of course he never gets — SOB!)

Likes: Fidgeting, break dancing, fancy ice cream
Dislikes: Flying, weak handshakes, AM radio

DANGEROUS DOT-TO-DOT

Grab a pencil and join the dots to discover who Howie's dangerous super-hero is.

Super-hero profile:

World's number-one stunting superstar

Home: Swed-o-vlakia

Personality: Fearless, always happy and smiling, enthusiastic

Superstition: Will not perform a stunt without Polka music blasting in the background

Likes: Stunting, Polka music, apple strudel

Dislikes: Romantic comedies, shopping, cold noodles

Turn to page 60 for the answer!

KITCHEN CHAOS SPOT THE DIFFERENCE

Piggy no like exploding jelly thing!

Poor Piggy has had a bit of a kitchen disaster. His giant Howieday jelly has exploded! Look at the two gooey pictures and see if you can spot 10 differences between them.

In addition to the 10 differences, Piggy has lost his special scoop in all the jelly mess. Can you help him find it?

Tick a jelly every time you spot a difference.

urn to page 60 for the answers!

WHO ARE YOU?

Take this crazy Cabana quiz to see which of the Almost Naked Animals you are most like. Turn to page 60 to find out the terrible truth!

Turn to page 60 to find out the terrible truth!

WARNING: Results may be surprising!

1. *A giant gorilla steals the big banana from the Cabana's roof. Do you ...*

   A Scratch your fleas and run in circles, while getting very excited at the thought of the dangerous adventure you can have getting back the banana?

   B Laugh maniacally — mwah ha ha! Perhaps now the rubbish hotel will have to shut down?

   C Cower in fear in a corner, as you worry about what terrible thing could happen next?

   D Cook a huge boogery banana cake in case the gorilla comes back to steal your bananas?

   E Put licorice in your navel and drink gravy?

   F Roll your eyes and wish that for just one day, you could work in a hotel where nothing went wrong?

   G Get up on the hotel stage and sing your favourite song — no gorilla is going to upstage you?

   H Sigh, swoon and not worry because you know that the love of your life will save the day?

2. *Someone has duck-napped Duck. Do you ...*

   A Plan a great rescue, the more dangerous the better?

   B Hope that your idiotic hench-animal has covered your tracks, because it was you who did the duck-napping?

   C Grab some plasters and hope that poor Duck hasn't been harmed, while desperately searching all the rooms in the hotel?

   D Grab your scoop and practise your kicks and karate chops?

   E Wonder where you are — perhaps you have gone into an alternate universe?

   F Feel huffy and shout at everyone to calm down, then take over the rescue plans?

   G Sigh, because you're going to miss your performance tonight if you have to help rescue him?

   H Ooze with support for the love of your life's great rescue plan?

3. Dirk Danger is holding auditions to find a sidekick for his new stunt movie. Do you ...

A Know that you are the best animal for the job, and dream of the joys of dangerous stunts?

B See it as an opportunity to close down your rival hotel?

C Become a jiggling mess because you just know that somehow you'll end up doing something dangerous?

D Plan the menu for the opening night movie party, while practising a few new ninjitsu moves?

E Eat a sandwich while standing on one leg?

F Ask the film director if there are any princess parts in the movie — you know you'd be brilliant?

G Ask the film director if you can sing the backing track for the movie?

H Keep your toes crossed in the hope that someone special in your life gets the starring role as Dirk's sidekick?

4. Somebody comes up with the idea of throwing a special surprise party for Piggy at the Banana Cabana. Do you ...

A Plan your most dangerous stunt yet as a party surprise?

B Sniff in disgust — you'd never willingly step foot in the Cabana or go to a party organized by Howie?

C Make a list of all the health and safety concerns that need addressing before the party can be held?

D Get suspicious that dog thing is up to something, and hope that it isn't a surprise for you because you hate surprises?

E Put on a party hat and get fun-kay?

F Try to take over the planning — after all, no one can organize a party like you can?

G Take a nap with cucumber slices on your eyes?

H Start getting ready the day before so that you stand some chance of getting to the party on time?

A DAY IN THE LIFE OF HOWIE

Howie the Hero

KAWOOOW!

Howie streaked across the sky, high above the Banana Cabana.

'YEARGGHHHHH!!'

It was turning into a pretty successful morning for Howie. He was testing out his Dirk Danger turbo-powered glider — and it was going brilliantly. So far, he'd only crashed twice, and he'd only hit himself on the head twelve times.

Far below, one of the hotel guests, Squirrel, was quietly reading a book.

'Ah, peace and quiet,' he said.

'YEARGH!!' Howie yelled, as he swooped over the pool and crashed through a pile of sun loungers, accidentally picking up Squirrel along the way.

'ARGH!' shouted Howie, as the glider rocketed up into the sky.

'Need some help?' shouted Squirrel, who was now holding on to the glider for dear life.

'Don't worry!' Howie shouted back. 'I've crashed lots of times before!'

'Crashed?!' cried Squirrel. 'Not on my watch!'

Squirrel had no time to lose. They were about three seconds away from some very large, very solid-looking trees. Trees that didn't look like they were about to move out of the way. But Squirrel was no coward.

'I've got you!' Squirrel shouted. He grabbed Howie's paw, and jumped from the glider.

'It's OK!' Squirrel yelled, as they fell through the air. 'You will land softly on your feet … Oh, wait. That's cats.'

A second later, Howie and Squirrel crashed into the ground — while the glider went flying headfirst into the trees and promptly exploded.

'That was AWESOME!' said Howie, grinning from ear to ear.

'And?' said Squirrel, frowning.

'Uh, and nice to meet you?' Howie asked, confused.

'No, you say …' Squirrel said, waiting for Howie to catch on.

'Nice to meet you …' Howie paused. 'Squirrel? You *are* a squirrel, right?'

'How about you say, "Thank you for saving my life!"?' Squirrel exclaimed.

Just at that moment, Howie's friend Octo came up behind them.

'What was that?' asked Octo. 'Did you just say: "Thank you for saving my life!"? Howie, you saved Squirrel! Howie — you're a HERO!'

'But—' said Howie. 'Wait! That's not what happened!'

But Octo couldn't hear him. Mainly because he was shouting:

'Howie! Howie! Howie's a hero! Howie's a hero!'

Soon everyone thought Howie was a hero. They gave him all the usual 'hero' presents: chocolate-covered marshmallows, and a huge hot air balloon shaped like his head. He even received the highest honour of all: peanut butter was renamed Howie Zowie Butter.

But Howie did not feel great. He knew he didn't really deserve to be called a hero. Then he had an idea. 'That's it!' Howie said. 'All I have to do is find Squirrel, put him in danger, try to rescue him, and then — if he lives — I'll be a real hero!'

So Howie raced to find Squirrel, and told him the plan. Soon, a reluctant Squirrel was standing on the roof of the Banana Cabana, just waiting for Howie to rescue him.

'Help,' he shouted. 'I'm in peril!'

Howie jumped into his new hot-air balloon, lifted off, steered it up to Squirrel — and rescued him off the roof … just before the balloon snagged on the giant banana on top of the Banana Cabana. And tore.

'Uh-oh,' said Squirrel.

'ARGHHH!' they both yelled, as the balloon whizzed madly around the sky.

'It's OK!' said Howie with a grin. He took Squirrel's hand, and jumped …

Squirrel and Howie landed on the ground. A little squashed, but safe.

'I saved you! I really saved you!' said Howie, jumping up and down. 'Now I AM a hero! Now you really *can* say, "Thank you for saving my life!"'

At that moment, Octo came up behind them. 'Howie, did I just hear you say: "Thank you for saving my life!"? Squirrel, you saved Howie's life!'

'Wait!' Howie tried to explain. But his voice was soon drowned out.

'Squirrel! Squirrel! Squirrel!' shouted Octo. 'Squirrel is a hero!'

'But — oh, never mind,' said Howie.

And he went off to enjoy some Howie Zowie Butter.

Which was, of course, now called Squirrely Whirly Butter.

TRUE OR FALSE?

Do you know your Cabana from your Chattoo? Take this test to find out whether you are more of a Banana brain or a Chateau clever clogs!

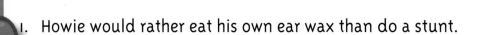

	TRUE	FALSE
1. Howie would rather eat his own ear wax than do a stunt.		✓
2. Poodle loves her brother, Howie.		✓
3. Octo spends most of his time worrying about health and safety.	✓	
4. As well as being a master chef, Piggy is a trained tuba instructor.		✓
5. Dirk Danger will not perform unless Polka music is playing.	✓	
6. Bunny thinks all of Howie's crazy plans are wonderful.		✓
7. Narwhal would happily look at himself in the mirror all day long.	✓	
8. Sloth has a huge crush on Piggy.		✓
9. Duck has a bunch of mini-Ducks, just like him … only mini-er.	✓	
10. Poodle's sidekick is called Potty.		✓
11. Howie never chases his own tail just for fun.	✓	
12. Poodle keeps a statue of herself in her office.	✓	
13. Poodle would do anything to shut the Banana Cabana down.	✓	
14. The Banana Cabana has a 5-star rating.		✓
15. Octo shares a room with Howie at the Banana Cabana.	✓	

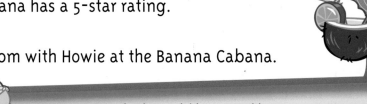

Turn to page 60 for the mind-blowing truth!

BUNNY'S WORDSEARCH

Bunny is the Banana Cabana's activities director. She has organized this mega wordsearch for you. Can you find all the words (listed below) in the grid? You'd better, otherwise Bunny will get very huffy — and that's not a pretty sight!

Words to find:

BANANA
BATTY
BEACH
BOOGERCHAIR
BUNNY

CABANA
CHATEAU
CHATTOO
DANGER
DIRK

DUCK
HOWIE
MANAGER
NARWHAL
NINJITSUCHEF

OCTO
PIGGY
POODLE
SLOTH
STUNT

When you've found all the words, colour in Bunny's pants.

C	H	A	T	T	O	O	D	M	A	N	A	G	E	R
H	O	N	X	N	B	T	B	Z	U	O	L	Y	V	K
A	P	K	H	I	Q	D	U	C	K	S	W	S	R	N
T	B	J	I	N	L	D	N	F	E	T	R	I	P	O
E	O	J	B	J	Q	W	N	S	P	U	D	V	B	R
A	H	H	P	I	G	G	Y	K	O	N	I	Y	N	I
U	O	E	R	T	H	M	S	L	O	T	H	K	L	A
S	W	Z	Q	S	E	G	Y	D	D	G	Y	P	O	H
V	I	T	F	U	Y	B	Z	B	L	N	D	O	L	C
A	E	C	A	C	G	T	E	C	E	B	Z	B	Q	R
T	R	Q	C	H	Z	O	B	A	N	A	N	A	K	E
D	A	N	G	E	R	O	E	B	U	B	H	T	P	G
I	S	Q	J	F	U	E	A	A	T	D	G	T	K	O
O	C	T	O	O	N	F	C	N	W	Z	V	Y	N	O
F	H	R	N	A	R	W	H	A	L	Y	U	G	O	B

21

Turn to page 61 for the answers!

HOWIE AND DUCK INTERVIEW ...

Narwhal is the Banana Cabana's resident performer and entertainer. He was the first (and only!) animal to apply for this job when the hotel opened. Now we've got exclusive access to his once-in-a-lifetime interview with Howie and Duck.

Q: Howie: I love doing dog things. What do you love doing?
A: Narwhal: Why, singing, of course, baby! Bop, bop, shu-waddy, doo, bop. My sultry tones will make you hop until you drop. You dig me?

Q: Duck: If you were a sandwich, what kind of sandwich would you be?
A: Narwhal: I'm thinking cheese, maybe with some peas, but then jelly would be yummy in your belly, if you get what I mean, baby! I'd certainly spread it with butter (boo-wop-da-doo), to make the lay-dees flutter!

Q: Howie: What's the most dangerous thing you've ever done?
A: Narwhal: Spent a whole day without looking in the mirror. That was one long, scary day.

Q: Duck: What is that pointy thing on your head?
A: Narwhal: That is my horn-o-rama. I polish it up every day. Why do you think I look sooooo good?

Q: Howie: When I'm not doing my managing stuff, I plan daring stunts. What do you do in your spare time?
A: Narwhal: Looking this good all the time takes a lot of work, so when I'm not crooning, I'm checking that this fish is still a dish!

Q: Duck: Sometimes I hear voices in my head.
 A: Narwhal: There's only ONE voice I want to hear in my head, baby … and it's mine! POW!

Q: Howie: I love to par-tay! Par-tay, par-tay, par-tay! What kind of party would you throw?
 A: Narwhal: Why, a butter one of course. That way we can all keep it buttery, baby.

Q: Duck: My favourite flavour is green.
 A: Narwhal: Uhm… Duck? That wasn't a question, baby.
 A: Duck: Agreed!

Q: Howie: I like to sing about bouncy things in the shower. What kind of songs do you sing?
A: Narwhal: I'll sing about anything you like, baby. How about, 'Wap wap weedle-op weedle-op wee, They put cheese all over me, well I danced with them and they danced with me, cheese on my knees!'

Q: Howie: Encore! Encore!
A: Narwhal: Shidly wat shidly wat shidly wat shilly, don't shave a banana with your eyes. It's a weird song, but that's all I got left!

CABANA CROSSWORD

If you're staying at the Cabana, we assume you like a bit of a challenge. So charge up those brain cells, work out the answers to the clues below and fill in this cool crossword. Just don't get your pants in a twist … after all, what could possibly go wrong?

Across

2) This little critter will do anything to win the approval of his evil boss. [5]
4) As well as being a master chef, Piggy is trained in this ancient martial art. [8]
7) If you're posh and like poodles, then get dialling and book a room here. [7,7]
9) Mirror, mirror on the wall, who is the greatest singer of all? [7]
10) You might want to clean your ears out, just don't tell Howie 'cos he loves this stuff. Yuck! [3,3]

Down

1) A top one-star establishment where you are guaranteed to have fun! [6,6]
3) The world's number one stunting action star. [4,6]
5) She may be super slow, but this doesn't stop this speed-challenged critter pursuing the love of her life. [5]
6) She will never get her paws dirty and she wonders how she can be related to a certain dog. [6]
8) Fizz ahoy! Who is the mascot of the gang's absolute favourite drink? [4,5]

Pssst! If you need a bit of help, the answers are on page 61. Not that we're suggesting you look — where would the fun be in that?

WHAT'S IN DUCK'S SHED?

What does Duck do when he's not fixing things in the Banana Cabana? No one really knows, but he does spend a lot of time in his shed. What does he get up to in there? Is it perhaps a portal to an alternate universe?

In the space below, draw what you think is in Duck's shed.

HOWIE

and

..........Alers,'s

ROOM

DO NOT ENTER
DANGEROUS STUNT IN PROGRESS!

HOWIE'S

HOTEL DOOR HANGER

HOWIE
and

..........Ben....'s

ROOM

ENTER
IF YOU WANT TO DO DARING DOG STUFF!

POODLE'S
HOTEL DOOR HANGER

POODLE

and

.....Kate.....'s

ROOM

ENTER ONLY IF
YOU HAVE
GIFTS FOR US!

POODLE

and

.....Sara.....'s

ROOM

DO NOT ENTER
UNDER ANY CIRCUMSTANCES IF YOUR
NAME SOUNDS LIKE 'OWIE'!
(YES, HOWIE, THAT MEANS YOU!)

I'D LIKE TO BOOK A ROOM AT THE BANANA CABANA!

Running a hotel like the Banana Cabana isn't an easy job.

Howie, erm, the lobby is overflowing with guests, erm, where am I going to put them all? I don't think we have enough rooms?

Recently, Howie got Duck to distribute Cabana room discount vouchers in town, and there has been a sudden rush of guests to the hotel.

Have you got the brain power to help Howie work out how he is going to accommodate all the guests, before Octo has a mega meltdown?

1. No vacancies! Octo needs to find space for 13 new guests, but he hasn't got any spare rooms. If 8 of these new guests are prepared to share rooms with existing guests, how many guests will Octo have to find extra space for?

2. 17 rooms are empty. There are 25 new guests desperately wanting rooms at the Cabana, and 11 current guests are just about to check out. If Octo checks in all of the new guests to separate rooms, how many empty rooms will he now have?

3. The next day, there are 7 rooms available. Octo has 11 new guests (Mammoth, Snake, Snail, Monkey, Kitty, Mole, Frog, Hedgehog, Anteater, Koala, Radiation Rooster) queuing at his desk. He can't put more than two guests in any of the rooms. Help him work out who to put in which room, if:

Mammoth is too big to share with anyone
Snake won't share with Frog or Snail
Kitty has said she'll share with Koala or Mole, but no one else
No one will share with Rooster because he's radioactive
Monkey will only share with Kitty or Anteater
Snail won't share with Hedgehog
Mole and Hedgehog will share with anyone but Snake
Koala will only share with someone who has requested it to be her
Snail gets on Frog's nerves

turn to page 61 for the answers ...

DON'T SPLIT YOUR PANTS LAUGHING!

Howie and the gang love a joke and a laugh.

Here are some of their favourite jokes. Read with caution, 'cos they're probably the funniest jokes you will ever hear!

Q: What did one flea say to the other flea?
A: *Shall we walk or take the dog?*

Knock, knock!
Who's there?
Howl!
Howl who?
Howl you know unless you open the door?

Q: Did you hear the joke about the broken egg?
A: *Yes, it cracked me up!*

Q: What do you get if you cross a cocker spaniel, a poodle and a rooster?
A: *Cockerpoodledoo!*

Q: What did the duck say after he went shopping?
A: *Put it on my bill!*
Q: Why was the bunny so upset?
A: *She was having a bad hare day!*

Q: Which circus performers can see in the dark?
A: *The acro-bats!*

Q: What dog likes to take bubble baths?
A: *A shampoodle!*

Q: Why did the banana go out with the prune?
A: *Because he couldn't find a date!*
Q: What do you give a sick pig?
A: *Oink-ment!*

Q: What time is it when a whale runs into your boat?
A: *Time to get a new boat!*

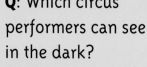

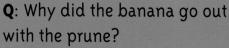

Q: What do you call a crate of ducks?
A: *A box of quackers!*

Q: Why did the narwhal cross the ocean?
A: *To get to the other tide!*

Q. What kind of key opens a banana?
A. *A monkey!*

What kind of book does a bunny like to read?
One with a hoppy ending!

Q: Why should Batty brush his teeth?
A: *Because he has BAT breath!*

Q. How do you know that carrots are good for your eyesight?
A. *Have you ever seen a bunny wearing glasses?*

Q. What do you give a dog with a fever?
A. *Mustard, it's the best thing for a hot dog!*

Q: What's a bunny's favourite music?
A: *Hip hop!*

Q: Why was the narwhal really disgusted?
A: *Because the sea weed!*

Q: What does an octopus wear on a cold day?
A: *A coat of arms!*

Q: Have you ever seen a fish cry?
A: *No, but I've seen a whale blubber!*

Knock, knock!
Who's there?
Banana.
Banana who?
Knock, knock!
Who's there?
Banana.
Banana who?
Knock, knock!
Who's there?
Orange.
Orange who?
Orange you glad I didn't say banana?

Q: What do you call a cat that swallows a duck?
A: *A duck-filled-fatty-puss!*

Q: Where do you find a dog with no legs?
A: *Where you left him!*

Q: What did the duck do after he read all these jokes?
A: *He quacked up!*

Q: Why don't bats live alone?
A: *They like to hang out with their friends!*

Story **by Richy K Chandler**   Art and Lettering **by Dill Tasker**

THE BANANA CABANA TOUR

Come and check out this year's most talked-about holiday destination, with me, Howie, your tour guide and manager of the ~~finest~~ *funnest* hotel on the entire beachfront.

Welcome to the Banana Cabana, home of an unidentifiable smell for the past three years!

Beachfront
Be sure to check out our world-class beach. We've only had two shark attacks in the last year.

Gazebo and pool area
Guests at our hotel always have plenty to do, thanks to our cool, calm and collected Activities Director, Bunny. (Exercise is optional, but if you want to keep in Bunny's good books, you'd better forget relaxing on our poolside loungers and get moving, pronto!)

Gym
Pump some iron in our superb in-hotel gym. Bunny will definitely approve of this activity.

Jacuzzi
Time to chill out with family and friends! (Pssst! Just don't let Bunny see you doing this.)

The Banana Cabana Lounge
Sink into a comfy chair with a cool drink or relax over dinner while listening to our very own resident star singer, Narwhal. Our light entertainment used to be every night, but now we've made it so it's NON-STOP, night and day, and night and day, and night and day...

The Banana Cabana kitchen

This fine establishment boasts a superb piggy-bleu menu cooked by our top master Ninjitsu chef, Piggy. And if you have food allergies, then no problem. NOTHING Piggy makes would even be considered food!

Rooms at the Banana Cabana

All our staff live at the hotel, so they can be contacted at any time. Check out these SWEET rooms. Look at that AWESOME bunk bed and all those toys and games. Of course this is just my room, which I share with Octo, but I'm sure your room will be nice too!

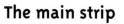

The main strip

A 5-minute walk from the hotel you'll find a good mix of shops and restaurants. Great for gift shopping — the staff love receiving presents — and sampling different cuisines (after you've eaten Piggy's food, you might want to eat out!). Try one of the famous Manicotti Mango bowls at the Fruity Noodle Hut, the most delicious restaurant around!

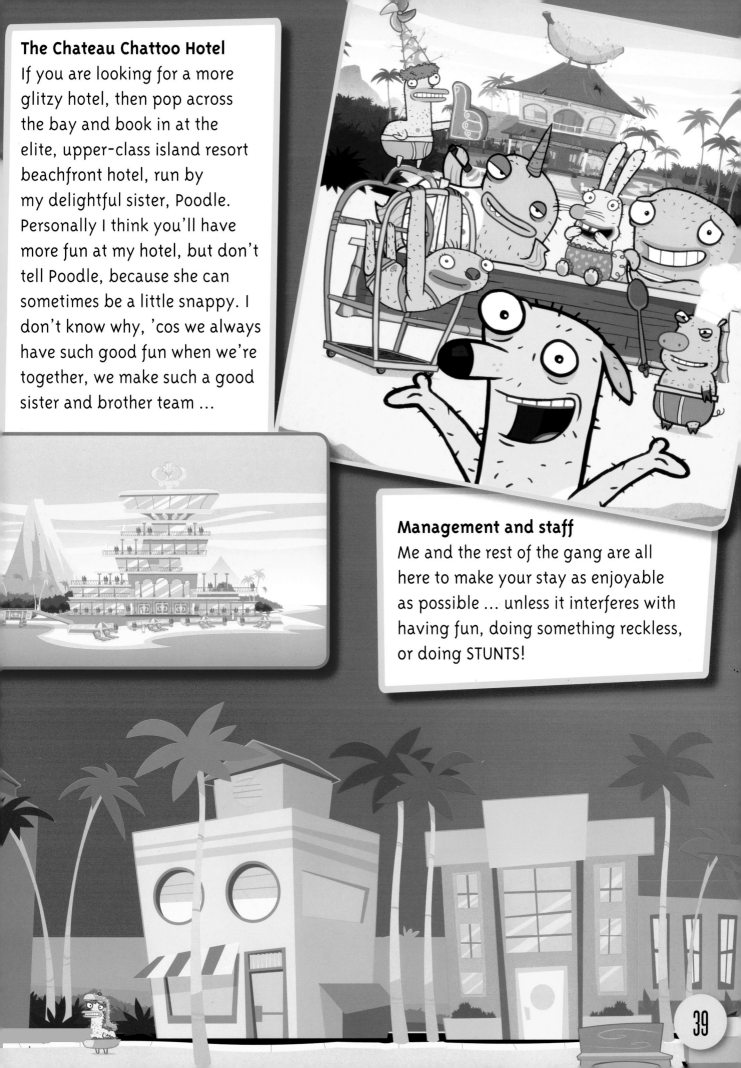

The Chateau Chattoo Hotel

If you are looking for a more glitzy hotel, then pop across the bay and book in at the elite, upper-class island resort beachfront hotel, run by my delightful sister, Poodle. Personally I think you'll have more fun at my hotel, but don't tell Poodle, because she can sometimes be a little snappy. I don't know why, 'cos we always have such good fun when we're together, we make such a good sister and brother team ...

Management and staff

Me and the rest of the gang are all here to make your stay as enjoyable as possible ... unless it interferes with having fun, doing something reckless, or doing STUNTS!

OCTO'S STUNT (AND EVERYDAY) SURVIVAL GUIDE

If, like me, you prefer to keep all your feet, paws, arms or claws firmly on the ground, and you don't like anything that is dangerous or scary, then this guide is for you. To all you stunt fanatics out there — you have been WARNED! If you choose to not follow these sensible guidelines, then I cannot be held responsible for any damage or pain that you experience! Believe me, there are dangers EVERYWHERE!

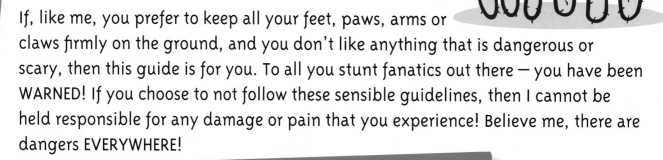

Octo's mottos:
You can never be too safe!
Safety first!
Is it safe enough?
Remove all possible causes of danger
from any given situation!
That looks the opposite of safe!
Octo's mission statement:
To make EVERYTHING safe and sound.

Survival Guide

1. Refuse to take part in any stunt if your friend keeps saying it isn't dangerous. Believe me, it will be dangerous.

2. Buy a first aid kit and make sure it is ALWAYS filled up with plasters and bandages.

3. Stock up on pillows — you can never have enough. Cover anything sharp or hard with them. They take the sting out of a 100-metre free-fall drop from a stunt bike.

5. If your friend starts waving a baseball bat around, saying 'What can possibly go wrong?', RUN as fast as all your legs will carry you.

6. Avoid doing any stunts in the dark. It can only end badly.

7. Relaxing on the beach — yes. Taking a safe and supervised little paddle in the sea — yes. Water skiing at top speed with your stunt fanatic friend — NO!!!

8. Whoever said clowns are funny, was WRONG, WRONG, WRONG! They are especially wrong if a stunt involves someone dressing up as one. To be avoided at all costs.

9. Now, it might seem like a relaxing way to spend a summer afternoon, floating gently, high in the sky, admiring the view … but if your friend says it would be fun to see how high you can float in a hot air balloon before leaping to the ground, then shake your head vigorously, smile politely and then RUN!

10. Stunts that involve runaway cars … do I really need to explain the dangers of this to you?

WHO TURNED THE LIGHTS OUT?

Where's Duck when you need him to change a light bulb? The Banana Cabana is in the dark … Howie accidentally smashed most of the hotel light bulbs while attempting to swing across the lobby ceiling! Using your superb powers of observation (and night vision goggles), can you match all the shadows below to the correct character? When you're done, you might want to go in search of Duck to light up the Cabana again.

Answers are on page 61.

WHOSE PANTS ARE THESE?

Arrgh! The Almost Naked Animals crew have got their pants in a right old twist! Can you sort out this mess and match each character with their own pants before they catch a chill?

WARNING: Some readers may find this activity mildly disgusting. Don't worry, just put on a pair of gloves and you'll be fine!

Which pair of pants are your favourite? Draw them here.

Answers are on page 61.

WHO SAID THAT?

How well do you think you know the crazy Almost Naked Animals gang? Are you bananas enough to match these sayings to their Cabana owners?

OKIE DONKEY!

I'LL GO GET MY FIRST AID KIT

I SCOOP YOU!

READY. SET. STUNT!

KEEP IT BUTTERY BABY!

WHAT COULD POSSIBLY GO WRONG?

Answers are on page 61.

PIGGY'S RECIPE

Spicy 12-Bean Kaboom Chili

WARNING: Do not attempt to make this chili at home — this speciality dish can only be made by super Ninjitsu chef Piggy!

Yee-haw! Howdy all bean-eating cowboys and cowgirls and, well, cows! Saddle up and ride on over to the Cowboy Cabana for some mighty fine bean chili. No one, and we mean NO ONE, makes a mean bean chili like Piggy — it's spicy, it's beany, and it'll have you parping and burping all over town!

RECIPE
Piggy's super spicy secret special sauce (including jar — it's the best part!)
5 tablespoons magic ninjitsu chili powder
Jar of jelly beans
Jar of Mexican jumping beans
Jar of black beans
Jar of green beans
Jar of navy beans
Jar of black-eyed peas
Jar of garbanzo beans
Jar of lima beans
Jar of soy beans
Jar of adzuki beans
Jar of mung beans
Jar of mesquite beans
2 jars of diced tomatoes
2 onions (whole)
Salt and pepper to taste

Pour all the ingredients into a large cauldron, mix well and stir over a high heat until bubbling like a volcano that's about to erupt!

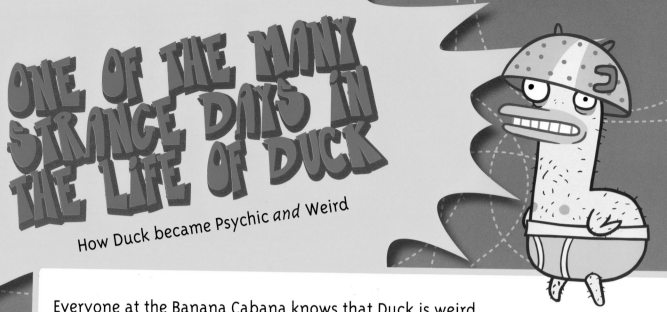

ONE OF THE MANY STRANGE DAYS IN THE LIFE OF DUCK

How Duck became Psychic and Weird

Everyone at the Banana Cabana knows that Duck is weird.

Weird enough that he can sing a single note for more than three hours. (I'm not saying it sounds good, but still).

Weird enough that he can play the musical saw (although not when the floor he's sawing through is out of tune).

Weird enough that he has a whole troop of mini-Ducks who act just as weirdly as he does (only smaller).

But he'll do anything for anyone, so there's always someone to invite for tea in his shed. They might even catch a glimpse of his booger chair.

Anyway, as everyone at the Banana Cabana knows, Duck is weird, and no one quite knows why. But they do know why he's psychic. That all happened one dark and stormy afternoon ...

'HELP!' yelled Howie. 'HELLLPP! DUCK!!'

It was raining buckets outside, all the lights had suddenly gone out at the Banana Cabana, and Howie was in a panic.

He ran. He shouted. He bumped into things. He yelled 'Duck!' until Duck came waddling to the rescue.

Soon, Duck was hammering at the Banana Cabana's giant fuse box, as the gang looked on, and thunder rumbled outside.

He was using his traditional tools: his pliers, his hammer, his screwdriver and his pineapple wrap. After a bit of tinkering, the lights flashed back on.

'Thanks a million, Duck!' said Howie. 'I knew that nothing bad could ever possibly in a million years *ever* go wrong!'

At precisely that moment, Duck held up his screwdriver, opened his beak to say something, and—

YEARGHHHHH!!!!

YEOUW!

Duck fizzed, turned upside down, fizzed some more, and then dropped on to the floor in a black, smouldering heap, as all his friends looked on in horror.

'Stay with me, buddy, you're going to be OK!' shouted Howie. Duck slowly lifted up his head and opened his eyes.

'You're alive!' said Howie. 'At least lightning never strikes twice in the same— YEARGHHH!'

Howie jumped in surprise, as a second, huge bolt of lightning struck Duck.

'YEOUUUWWWW!' yelled Duck, as his eyes spun dizzily in his head. His beak crackled. His feet fizzed. And as the bolt of lightning went through him, Duck spun round and round, until he finally landed on the floor with black clouds of smoke rising from his head.

'Duck?' said Howie. 'Duck, are you ...'

Everyone gasped, as Duck slowly stood up, blinked, and looked around him.

'Bouncy landings make happy endings,' said Duck.

'Well, whatever you say. The important thing is you're alive!' said Howie.

'Travelling rodents mean you harm,' said Duck.

'He sounds ... like a fortune cookie,' said Howie. 'Duck, what's my fortune?'

'Something you lost will soon turn up,' said Duck.

And right on cue, Howie turned around, and found the lollipop he'd lost earlier, stuck to his tail.

As Howie tucked in to his lollipop, the still-smouldering Duck waddled off.

'There's something *weird* about Duck,' said Bunny.

'He's not weird!' said Howie. 'He's just psychic!'

Bunny and Howie both looked over at Duck, who was quietly humming a tune and dancing on a table, while balancing a pineapple on his head.

Dancing slowly, Duck wandered off towards his shed.

'Maybe you should follow him, just to make sure he's really OK,' said Bunny.

'Yeah … maybe,' said Howie.

Howie thought back to the last time he had strayed into Duck's shed, and shivered.

Was that really a, a, a, you know? Howie thought with a gulp. *And did I really see a – one of those in there? And those things – they … couldn't really have been, you know – them?? Could they?*

'I think I'll er, just leave Duck to rest for now,' said Howie.

And so Duck spent the rest of the afternoon, happily inside his shed. He quietly predicted the future, as he conducted his mini-Duck orchestra. Which was both psychic *and* weird.

HOW TO DRAW DUCK

Grab a pencil and your favourite coloured pens, and follow these simple steps to draw the Banana Cabana's particularly peculiar handy animal, Duck.

Step 1

Draw the outline as shown below, leaving a space for Duck's beak.

Step 2

Add in Duck's beak, teeth and legs.

Step 3
Finally, draw Duck's pants, add some hairs and colour your picture.

Here are some accessories that Duck might wear or use. Once you feel confident drawing Duck, draw him as many times as you want to, on your own pieces of paper and give him some of these items to wear.

CHATEAU CHATTOO CODEBREAKER

What is that sneaky princess pooch, Poodle, up to?

Use the alphabet code below to work out the secret message that Poodle has sent to her right-paw animal, Batty.

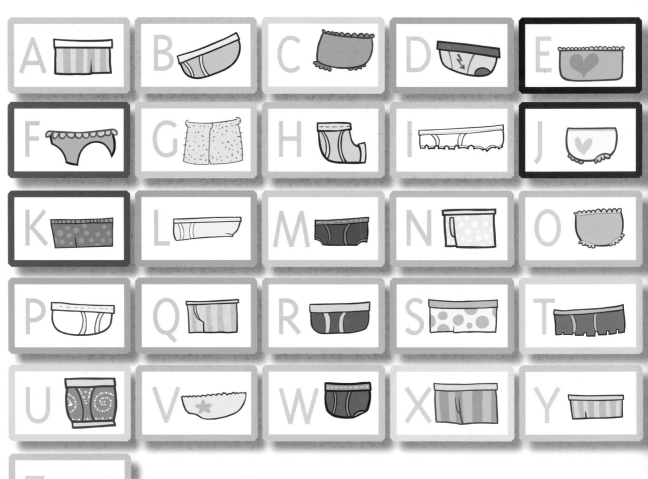

Once you have cracked the code, why not try using it to write your own secret messages to your friends?

meet   me   On

Beach   at   noon

FOr   OPERaTiOn

CaPang   ,   shuT DOwn

DON T   Be   Late

!

Batty   ohhohh
                        evils

The answer is on page 61!

WHODUNNIT?

Be afraid, be very afraid. Piggy no like cake thief thing!

Piggy very not happy because some thing has eaten the cake he's just spent all morning baking.

Read the clues below to see if you can work out whodunnit. Hurry, though, 'cos Piggy looks like he might explode, or karate-chop someone with one of his super cool ninjitsu moves.

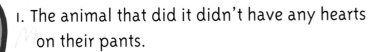

'It wasn't me, honest. Ooh, I feel a bit dizzy! I think I need to sit down.'

1. The animal that did it didn't have any hearts on their pants.

2. It definitely wasn't the animal that doesn't like taking long walks, or any walks for that matter.

3. The animal that spent the morning staring in the mirror couldn't have done it.

4. It couldn't have been the animal that spent the morning at the Chateau Chattoo with his sister.

5. The animal who loves herself more than anyone else would have taken it in a flash, but she was too busy buffing her toenails.

6. There was a suspicious trail of cake crumbs leading out of the hotel towards a small building at the back of the hotel.

7. The animal who is afraid of his own shadow couldn't have done it because he would have been too scared.

The answer is on page 61!

ALMOST NAKED ANIMALS SUDOKU

It might not be dangerous, but it certainly is a challenge! Are you up for it? Finish this tricky Sudoku puzzle by filling in the blank squares with the correct Almost Naked Animals character.

Remember, each of the six characters must appear only once on each horizontal and vertical line.

Find the answer on page 61!

HOWIE'S DOG THING

Most of the time Howie doesn't have much on his mind apart from doing stunts … and then a couple more stunts! It's a dog thing! Look at the image in the grid and then copy each part of it into the grid below, to complete your own picture of the carefree canine. Colour your picture and then go and chase your tail for a while. Trust us, it's fun!

HEY! THAT'S MINE!

Ahhhhh! What's going on? Bunny is shouting at everybody. Octo is quivering and jittering in a corner. And Piggy is ninjitsu-chopping everything he comes into contact with.

We should've guessed. Howie has been practising another one of his stunts in the hotel lobby and now the Cabana crew's belongings are all over the place. Can you help them tidy the place up by matching each character to their stuff? Hurry, Bunny is getting THAT LOOK in her eye! Answers can be found on page 61 …

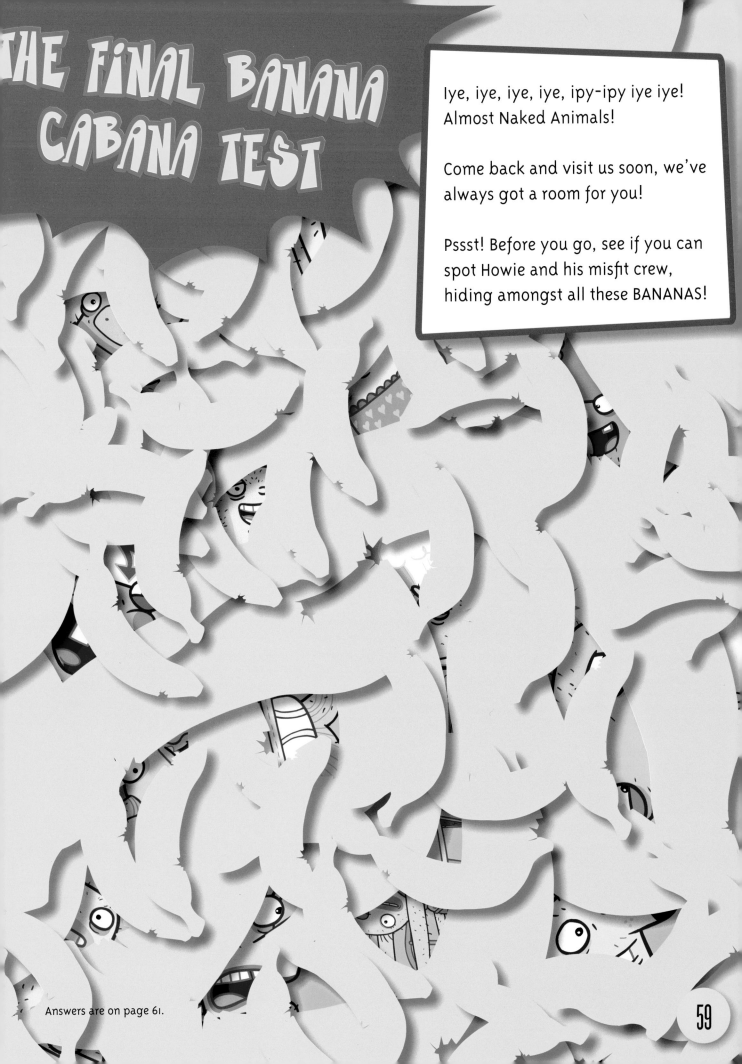

THE FINAL BANANA CABANA TEST

Iye, iye, iye, iye, ipy-ipy iye iye! Almost Naked Animals!

Come back and visit us soon, we've always got a room for you!

Pssst! Before you go, see if you can spot Howie and his misfit crew, hiding amongst all these BANANAS!

Answers are on page 61.

ANSWERS

Duck in his hero sandwich
outfit appears eight times in this Annual!

p13
Dirk Danger is Howie's hero.

p14/15

pp16/17
Mostly As: Howie; Mostly Bs: Poodle; Mostly Cs:
Octo; Mostly Ds: Piggy; Mostly Es: Duck; Mostly Fs:
Bunny; Mostly Gs: Narwhal; Mostly Hs: Sloth

p20
1. False! Howie would always prefer a dangerous stunt over almost anything else.

2. False! Poodle can't stand her goof-ball brother!

3. True! If poor old scaredy-pus Octo didn't have something to worry about, then you can guarantee that he would be behind the front desk, quivering and shaking, worrying that he didn't have anything to worry about!

4. False! Piggy really no like the noise of shiny noisy thing. This master chef would rather be practising his ninjitsu moves!

5. True! Surprisingly for someone who loves danger, the number-one stunter in the world is incredibly superstitious. He will not perform a stunt unless his beloved Swed-o-vlakian Polka music is playing.

6. False! Bunny definitely has her own ideas about how things should be done around the Banana Cabana!

7. True! He can think of nothing more fascinating than staring at his own handsome reflection.

8. False! She only has eyes for one creature, and that's her beloved Howie. Ahhh … how sweet!

9. True! Why wouldn't he?

10. False! Poodle would never employ anyone called Potty! Batty is the name of her sidekick. A much more appropriate name, don't you think?

11. False! Tail chasing is near the top of Howie's list of things he loves to do!

12. True! Who else would Poodle have a statue of in her own office?

13. True! The day the Banana Cabana shuts down will be the best day EVER as far as Poodle is concerned.

14. False! Unfortunately the hotel star-rating board does not give out stars for FUN. If they did, the Banana Cabana would receive the top rating!

15. True! Octo and Howie are best friends.

p21

C	H	A	T	T	O	O	D	M	A	N	A	G	E	R		
H	O	N	X	N	B	T	B	Z	U	O	L	Y	V	K		
A	P	K	H	I	Q	D	U	C	K	S	W	S	R	N		
T	B	J	I	N	L	D	N	F	E	T	R	I	P	O		
E	O	J	B	J	Q	W	N	S	P	U	D	V	B	R		
A	H	H	P	I	G	G	Y	K	O	N	I	Y	N	I		
U	O	E	R	T	H	M	S	L	O	T	H	K	L	A		
S	W	Z	Q	S	E	G	Y	D	D	G	Y	P	O	H		
V	I	T	F	U	Y	B	Z	B	L	N	D	O	L	C		
A	E	C	A	C	G	T	E	C	E	B	Z	B	Q	R		
T	R	Q	C	H	Z	O	B	A	N	A	N	A	K	E		
D	A	N	G	E	R	O	E	B	U	B	H	T	P	G		
I	S	Q	J	F	U	E	A	A	T	D	G	T	K	O		
O	C	T	O	O	N	F	C	N	W	Z	V	Y	N	O		
F	H	R	N	A	R	W	H	A	L	Y	U	G	O	B		

p29

1. 5
2. 3

3. Room 1 Mammoth
   Room 2 Snake
   Room 3 Radiation Rooster
   Room 4 Kitty, Koala
   Room 5 Monkey, Anteater
   Room 6 Frog, Hedgehog
   Room 7 Mole, Snail

pp24/25

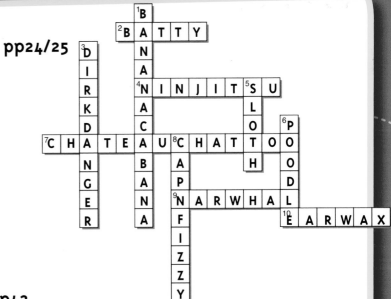

(Crossword)
1. BANANA
2. BATTY
3. DIRKDANGER
4. NINJITSU
5. SLOTH
6. POODLE
7. CHATEAU
8. CHATTOO / CHAPBANANAFIZZY
9. NARWHAL
10. EARWAX

p42

a-8, b-7, c-5, d-4, e-6, f-2, g-3, h-1.

p43

a-7, b-6, c-8, d-11, e-12, f-1, g-5, h-10. i-2, j-9, k-4, l-3.

p44

Howie: 'What could possibly go wrong?'
Octo: 'I'll go get my first aid kit.'
Duck: 'Okie Donkey!'

Narwhal: 'Keep it buttery, baby!'
Piggy: 'I scoop you!'
Dirk Danger: 'Ready. Set. Stunt!'

pp52/53

MEET ME ON BEACH AT NOON FOR OPERATION CABANA SHUTDOWN. DON'T BE LATE, BATTY!

pp54/55 Duck is the cake thief thing!

p58

Howie: Dirk Danger toy/Skates
Octo: First aid kit
Piggy: Spoon/Hat/Saucepan
Duck: Hat/Plunger/Foam hand
Bunny: Princess outfit/Sunglasses
Narwhal: Microphone

p59

Batty, Bunny, Cap'n Fizzy, Cockroach, Octo, Dirk Danger, Piggy, Narwhal, Duck, Sloth, Poodle and Howie.

p56

2	6	3	1	5	4
1	5	4	6	2	3
5	2	1	4	3	6
3	4	6	2	1	5
6	3	2	5	4	1
4	1	5	3	6	2

1 = 2 = 3 = 4 = 5 = 6 =